Poetry Garden

where every poem tells a story

Written By,
Trinankur Bera

Poetry Garden

Copyright © Trinankur Bera 2020.
All rights reserved.
Originally published in 2020.
No part of this publication may be reproduced, stored in a retrieval system, or transmitted in any form or by any means without the prior permission in writing of the author, nor be otherwise circulated in any form of binding or cover. It would be breach of copyright to reproduce any of these poems on paper or online without my permission.

About the book : from the author

In this work there are fifteen poems and a few reflections.The poems are broader in structure due to its immense resemblance to a story.

Every poem holds a different story knitted in the form of a poem. If read with the patience of a story the best from them can be extracted.
The musings at the last phase of the book reflect certain aspects of life in a few words.
I dedicate this book to all of it's readers with love and respect.

(Trinankur Bera)

About the Author:

Trinankur is an engineer from kolkata,India who likes to weave stories from his creativity.He dreams of becoming a respected writer and do great things for this world.He hopes that his broad poem structure in this book will still be enjoyed by most in this busy lifestyle.

Author's email id:trinankur.45@gmail.com

Contents

poetry garden	Pages
The distant member	1-2
The mother's stunt	3-5
The diamonds we left behind	6-9
The midnight craving	10-12
The rays of prejudice	13-15
Mucu the canine	16-17
The house in Middleton	18-22
After a long time	23-26
The chauffeur,the human	27-30
The departed	31-32
Disloyal to nature	33-37
The forever strings	38-40
The game of possessions	41-45
The gift of snow	46-49
It doesn't belong here	50-52
A tub of reflections	1-8

Poetry Garden

The distant member

Phase-1

I meet you again,
after counting a year in a row of ten.
A lie it will be,
if I say I didn't think about you.

Your face, your voice was prominent,
like the moon on its brightest time.
I had hope I would meet, one day.

Been carrying your gift all this time,
in my wallet.
That day nothing I had to gift you
except a warm hug, of those adolescent arms.

Phase-2

I vowed that day I would buy something lovely
only for you from my first earning.
Honestly, I did not recognize you,
when I bumped into the seat beside.

page-1

Poetry Garden

But the same freshly brewed brown in the eyes,
the same pentagon in the chain,
slipping down the neck.
It struck me like a reckless storm from south
just in the midway of my ingress.
When that reluctant hug came up,
I knew you remembered it all,
just like I do.

Maybe we went to different families
who provided the love we prayed for,
every single day.

I prayed that someplace, somewhere
may our path's collide,
to give me back my first sister
I made in that orphanage.

Poetry Garden

The mother's stunt

Phase-1

In my fathomed evening blues, drenched,
slowly climbed the stairs to cleanse it away
to taste a little, the stranger winds passing by.

Climbing was so tough at the time,
just took a seat by the wall to unwind.
The flock of cranes flew like an arrow head,
making a sound so serene, depicted the dusk.
The orange turned to dark with starry spots.

And the clouds vanished somewhere in between,
the strangers came less frequent,
blessed the child and moved along the way.
The moon in vague could be seen,
waiting for darkness to settle him in.

Poetry Garden

About time to go back to my room
when a sound came, very unfamiliar yet strong it was.
A pouncing sound came from the chimneys dark.

I reached for the iron bar,
abandoned was it till then,
I peeked while one hand above the baby,
unconsciously,
I found a dark, furry animal.
With the flourishing fall of darkness,
still was I sure to had found a racoon.

Phase-2

No clue I had for its mere presence.
It went upside down,
while the tail still visible like an epitome.
Soon it came out, but with a baby.
it was 'her' indeed,
a new member of the mothers.
She found this marvellous place,
which could keep her baby
warm and safe all together.

Poetry Garden

As she climbed down,
her baby grasped in her mouth.
Something urged me from the inside.
I engaged, my body yet defensive
in contradict my mind.

Such a dangerous path it was.
Just so the baby can feel the land in her feet.
She thought it was worth it
to teach all that she knew,
and wave the fur as it grew.

She gave me a lot that day,
courage and strength indeed,
to embrace you and give you my all,
to erase all problems with your giggle of stall.
Maybe she breathed me that day.
She knew that a to be mother,
might use some help.

Poetry Garden

The diamonds we left behind

Phase-1

Been a month few.
Familiar faces, mostly.
Same grills of rust and seats weary by the window.
The whistling wind with the galloping,
the perfect song it leaped for time travel.

The mornings were much serene, sunny.
After dusks brought too much rush.

I was staring at the sparks of sun.
On the watch, sometimes on floor,
a man sat beside, very different,
too neat, much classy in attire,

greeted me with a smile,
much brighter than the morning.
And bowed a little forward,
a little courtesy shown, long lost in race.

Poetry Garden

Phase-2

Flipped open his briefcase brown,
and bounded open his newspaper,
wide enough, entire row could grasp words.
He waved through pages trying to find
something the mood found worth reading.
Thus I concluded, in blur.

More focused I was on his subtle shoes,
just when we paused at the station fifth,
a lady came and grasped the steel.
She looked young and pale,
the guy without thinking smiled again,
and gifted his seat.
No, wrong I was to assume he was plotting
to flash a conversation.
He was just finely blended
of kind and generous.

Many thought he was just showing
off as we say.
But they were astonished like me to witness.
I noticed his wrists had no watch.
Maybe he forgot.

Poetry Garden

But in a minute he pulled out something,
much extraordinary from his overcoat,
a golden pocket watch resplendent,
contrasting his vibrant grey fit.

He still had the confidence to use
with such excellence,
in such a place of change unbound.

Phase-3

He anchored, two stations before mine,
I just wished I would see more of him,
rather humanity.

But again I saw him on a Monday,
while trying to jerk off the weekend aura,
same guy, same affable smile.
But o dear!.Stains of dark,
spit on his shoes.

Poetry Garden

On enlightened he did not failed to astonish,
just shrugged, laughed and threw the paper,
which he tore to clean it fine.

Soon I discovered he choose to board,
different bogeys in line.
Maybe to showcase his biggest asset,
of humanity and courtesy,
hoping to inflict if he might.
One day I gathered the courage to ask.
He told "Larry is my name and I chose
not to return to my time".

Poetry Garden

The midnight craving

Phase-1

Night before, woke up all startled.
I could feel a craving in my mouth,
for a very unique taste.

Unable to reminisce,
just sipped some water from the glass beside,
but the craving was still so alive,
in a constant endeavour.
I felt strange, knew perfectly how it should taste,
should begin like a sweet muffin
and mould into unsalted butter.

Was about to get off bed,
to be a less form of uncertain.
I was to found a lot of medications crowding,
just beside the lamp.
A strip I took and studied it under the light,
to have found the reason.

Poetry Garden

The word Alzheimer flashed through my mind
to yield off my reason.
The reminder of disabilities
left me deserted,
Drabbing my composure.

The tears came rushing,
to wash the sullied dejection,
and calm me to let sleep walk inside.
Unnoticed it went,
when did Louisa got awake.

Phase-2

She guessed half of the reasons of tears mine,
knowing the medicine in my hand,
she put her warm palms on my face
and kissed me with a essence of affection.

Poetry Garden

I met again, I found the zest I was looking for,
all this while.
It was something,
never to forget in the real world.

It was but Louisa's lips I was rummaging for.
No doubt I remembered.
Only but the marvellous touch of the rare craving.

Poetry Garden

The rays of prejudice

Phase-1

Announced were the dates.
To cast our votes and gift the stage.
To let become a gallant and serve the world,
to be praised for life, and beyond.

Rallies began and sailed through the roads.
Emerged the emblems from them,
hoisted in the air,
wavering similar to a king's fort.

Echoed the slogans,
profound even to the forbidden rooms,
walls on the road screamed or scoffed the other.
As the dates scuttled along,
the happening can be felt all around.

Like a fete under hustle,
one voice, one face familiar,
stood out in his grandeur.
No, not a leader,

just another bearer of the flag,
trying in every way to provide,
devoted to just be a part of it.

Poetry Garden

When door to door he went,
delivering crisp envelops mostly in white and brown.
Other days just found painted,
in his colour of pride,

tried to dissuade him,
only his peers.
to use his work and leave some words behind.
But firm he was in the armour of ideals.

Phase-2

An afternoon, all sultry and emphatic,
he paddled among the antagonized walls.
While soaking his face of sweat
he was stopped, just crossing the enclave.

Poetry Garden

He tried to masterly elude as the thrashing began,
they knew no mercy.
But he failed as he began to bleed.
The wounds started to appear
and followed into the sack torn.
In agony he fainted and was left,
when threatened the mob felt.
Rescued he was on time.
The red stained envelops flew back.

When he set his foot again,
on the road to return home,
he felt reborn, he felt translucent,
And most unpredictably, even surprising himself,
he felt joy.

Such an intrepid was born that day,
no one would have known.
the inhuman beating, the pain,
the incident.
All would evanesce.
If not the envelopes were finally delivered.
unaltered, with dried taints.

Poetry Garden

Mucu the canine

Phase-1

Mucu came when he was needed, most.
Amidst the clouds of my despondent feelings,
just like an archangel.
He has a forest of fur when fondled,
can calm all storms.
The eyes to deep dive and find crystals of peace.

Mucu is my extraordinary black retriever.
Before I met him by fate,
never realized that black could be so beautiful.

The most docile you can ever ask for.
And the magic that is,
mother has not complained of his first visit.
From a place he belongs where they have every colour
and every breed.
So everyone can have 'mucu',
in just the way they love.

Phase-2

No, you never have to worry about him.
Never will he give a chance to worry.

Poetry Garden

Never will he leave.
If you just seek for him, time to time.
Delusional yet Mucu is one of the immortals.
Brought Mucu from a galaxy of creations.
I impulsively brought him here for one reason,
just to survive the storms.
But he prized with two more,
to live life and laugh a little more.

Poetry Garden

The house in Middleton

Phase-1

Never were we really constant,
to a locale,
when ambience finally tried to befriend us,
we abandoned her.
Embraced in sorrow and guilt,
father brought the news in a evening faded.
The order had arrived to sail to a island new.

Yet we grasped everything and went aloof.
But vividly divergent was the house last.
A whole of third floor flat,
windows on faces both, to soak in more.

I took the roadside room,
a clear choice for a modern child,
to check, urban buzzing.

Paddling across the road stood a banquet,
emerged like a royal possession.
I couldn't recall to have seen something alike.
So much happened every time I peeked,almost.

Poetry Garden

Everytime dressed up,
ornamented in a pinch of difference.

The smell of delicacies whiffed with the evening fall.
People bright and shiny filled the lawn.
Entrapped them with varieties and no menu,
ladle's always reluctant in their grandeur.

And the shiny baskets, plates half filled
heaped along.
Sometimes I would down the room light
and just ponder.

Phase-2

Past a week shifted to the guest room.
With a promising deal,
to shift back just when the paint is slick,
Never really fathomed that room
since we tented.
Very distinct yet a transparent picture,
drew from the window.

Poetry Garden

An enclave poor,
where the sun seemed stronger than any other.
Very vivid, a small marred room in sight.
beautifully turned to be a house of three.
The wind much humid but strong,
wavered the curtain soiled.
To reveal the child in bounded privation.
Holding his toy with his subtle eyes

came his father looking enough drained,
torn slippers and a shirt to fray.

sat beside pacing his hands through his young's hair.
Then came one lunch on the mother's hand.
Only the rice to clearly see,
remarkably mocking a white ants den.

That was all to come, to feed upon.
Two hands working mirrored on it,
while the mother embellished for the kid.
Making lunch fun a play,

I withdrew my eyes and gazed
on the side other of the room.

Poetry Garden

Phase-3

Overwhelmed with a storm of feelings,
reminded of the last night's plates,
the leap of food willing to waste.
Droughts of gratitude slowly giving way,

for a moment I felt like abolishing,
the whole of my house.
And break through the walls
to make them see the extreme painting of today,
and scream "yes please carry on!".

While the lanterns of humans drown.
"Oh! yes please carry on!".
Better teach our children now.
How the lines imaginary work.
Of big and small, of more and less.
Or show mercy to the light and let it come,
And bloom with care while we still can.

Poetry Garden

After a long time

Phase-1

The phone doesn't sleep much now.
Work demands and thus I need it, awake.
With a gift it comes perhaps.
My women feels more calm.
Like quite distant from a bee swarm.

New is the job and it feels like to stay.
For the first time the two have hold hands.
At least I get to music the strings,
with the ones to love.
That being, the most costly.
Where you have time, for you.

After a few stops when it feels done is the suffering,
I plug in my songs, always inclined to the wheel of mood.
Sometimes comes a feeling of unique dimension.
But when it floats up on my face,
the mirrored person mostly looks away.
I am habituated, adapted,
that people don't connect as often.

Poetry Garden

Phase-2

I am fortunate to have found a connection,
who accepts my all.
We swirl through movies, we dine out.
But every Sunday night the ceiling tells me,
"You missed again".

I feel a taint of stress, maybe which wasn't swayed.
But I have done, what people do for recreation,
haven't I.

Walking through the pavement once, she noticed
the small stream of gloominess dissenting.

We sat on a marble stair,
waving white stairs of a store.
While I held her hand and took her to the swell
which was unknown to me on my favourite wall.
Worried, deep she seemed.

Then with a smirk peaking from her face,
she fenced me with her hands.
And whispered "I might just solve this case".

Poetry Garden

Tried to sneak in sometimes with a curious wit.
But she won't let me in.
Well soon it faded.

About four in the morning it was,
I checked with my cloudy eyes.
It was her name flashing among the dark.

Her voice with a hue of stress when she spoke.
I scuttled putting on my shoes, giving a hint to father.
The thought of her twisted knee caged me.

I reached in a minutes few,
on the pale brown wood she sat, she seemed fine.
I stood on other side, staring in disbelief.
When she came running from the shack
while hate spilled from me within.
And she whispered, "I am sorry, come with me".

Phase-3

She engaged, not hesitating
to touch my sweaty hands.
On the field we sat,
While the nifty grass tickled in our bare foot.

Poetry Garden

Tried to sneak in sometimes with a curious wit.
But she won't let me in.
Well soon it faded.

About four in the morning it was,
I checked with my cloudy eyes.
It was her name flashing among the dark.

Her voice with a hue of stress when she spoke.
I scuttled putting on my shoes, giving a hint to father.
The thought of her twisted knee caged me.

I reached in a minutes few,
on the pale brown wood she sat, she seemed fine.
I stood on other side, staring in disbelief.
When she came running from the shack
while hate spilled from me within.
And she whispered, "I am sorry, come with me".

Phase-4

She engaged, not hesitating
to touch my sweaty hands.
On the field we sat,
While the nifty grass tickled in our bare foot.

Poetry Garden

She cuffed her fingers to mine
and her body lazy towards me.
I calmed all, as the light breeze kissed on the neck.
Embraced her with one hand.
while the small kids started to unpack.

Feeling the ground, the soil,
sweeping the grass with bare foots.
This is what I missed.
A very small fragment of life,
yet the most vivid one.
She was right.
I missed the nature, I missed my field.
After a long time I felt like a being, more like I felt human.
After a long time.

Poetry Garden

The chauffer, the human

Phase-1

Still I remember how I glared at it,
every morning.
I thought of it as the most valuable,
among all we possessed.
The car was our gravity in family.
So yellow and bright it shined when I boarded.
I felt so at grace and much elated.

Being the first passenger of the drive, days most,
what a splendid job father had!.I thought to myself.
In the age of simple,
for every peer it was T for train,
but I loved T for taxi, redundantly.

Monday it was, somewhere in my memories,
a little blurry but yet constant.
Emphatic I was for school that day,
but they won't let me go, not safe.

```
Poetry Garden
```

Phase-2

Everything flurried the same to me.
The yellow ride, father,
all were on course.
Impulsively I made a mistake, adolescent.
Exposed, when an uncle known came inside.
I sat up with guilt, peeking at father.

A pace of many emotions hovering through his face.
I didn't knew it's meaning much.
He said none and just drove.
His shirt slowly getting sullied
by the thoughts.
Streets were so empty, so wide numb.
It was not just another day.

Just as soon as uncle wavered his gratitude,
meeting his stop.
Father raced the car the other way.
Just enough fast,
to beat my hands with the orange toy car.

Poetry Garden

When I thought to let the plea spring,
"Pull up the windows and don't to dare open it"
came the voice.

The whistling of the wind faded.
Just sound of the engine from one open
of father's side.
Only the sun flickering it's light inside,
playing with the buildings all.

Dashed in a stone from a gathering,
hollering from the other side,
they held flags in quintessence
like the pirate ships in my book.

Father blocked his wound with one red cloth.
Hard to tell how much he bled.
Still firm and steady commanding the wheel.

Phase-3

The same evening I sneaked in again.
This time beside him, lying on the bed
trying to sleep.

```
Poetry Garden
```

A white band around his forehead,
with a red spot glowing from it,
asked "Why were you hit? Did you bend any rules?"
Not understanding, much like a fool,

he reached my one hand and said
"I just don't have a job they can respect".
Father after so many years I hope to see you,
maybe among the clouds.
When today I will take many to their destinations,
just like you.
Operating, from the cockpit.

Poetry Garden

The departed

Phase-1

Today, we proudly glare at our beautiful creation.
A few seats in between for separation.
Confused the little soul from the stage,
Whom to look at?
To fill the confidence tray.

There she danced like a butterfly in sunshine,
a new feeling of joy and sorrow combined.
I looked across the line to take a glimpse of your face,
to make a path for emotions to find their twin to pray.

The path took me into the memories locked in despair.
The bright memories of you again seemed like my own sapphire.
From the first time I saw you dance in that yellow silk.
To the time I witnessed that cute little thing
sleeping on your chest.

Could again connect with every beautiful fragment, of your love.
Not for a moment it felt we have departed long enough.

Poetry Garden

Phase-2

Snap! the memories vanished in fear.
The sound of the claps brought me back in my chair.
There stood my little girl bowing in gratitude,
Her mother with the loudest claps
feeling proud in solitude.

Them again in the hallway I saw.
Her mother wiping off the make-up
before her prize call.

Soon the resplendent eyes fell upon me,
and she came running.
Wrapped me in those small hands
and kissed right on my cheek.
But soon my little moon went away with her guardian,
to stir me of the precious things lost.
I being the lonely one now,
could not even howl my affection.

Poetry Garden

Disloyal to nature

Phase-1

Owned the sail all by himself.
Just like another fisher yet he went along.
Every morning, pondered the above.
His eyes restless, his senses evolved.
As if he could speak to travellers of the sky
coming home from sky of the sea.

Little late brother would rise.
Prepare for the rendezvous awaits.
If my senses hit, fiercely I would beg.
Take me along thus the only uttered phrase.

I would be told, It's not yet time,
would be taken when age has climbed.
After a few years I was offered to tag.
Without the begging and the fierce nag.
But in seldom the chances came.

Poetry Garden

Made the most of it, grasped all I could,
the winds of ocean crashed through my soul,
to look at the never ending blue horizon
and feel blessed.
The coat of green would make the boat
into an island so small.

Phase-2

First day, when the fishes were being stacked
sounds of a airgun dropped me to hide,
was conciliated to be brought outside.
And told to peer at the walls of our sail.
Along the waves of the hitting stash,
Stood a bottle nosed dolphin.

Spouting water jets and making goofy sounds.
The one who was behind the scaring.
Ate all the fishes threw on him.
Never failing to clutch on.
What a marvellous creature I thought.
Having witnessed for the first.

Soon it was known, that he can recognize.
The boat and thereby us too.

Poetry Garden

More fond this gesture made of me.

With the growing age of the year,
the bond has mounted as well.
He would now swing in the air,
to let us feel with touch and play along.

Though scarce I felt for fishing
often would I sail, to meet,
scared of him the school's often rush,
and end up being trawled all together.
Rewarded he would be with more of food,
what a show he would make.

One day caught it was in my eyes,
throwing cans of soda, my own brother to fight,
relentless he seemed from my words ungentle.
'Nothing so little can harm this vast ocean!'.
Yet I begged, not to forward.
In school that week such things were taught.

The next few days were confined.
Rushing was a storm to batter our doors.

Poetry Garden

Of all the time spent, it came in midnight
strong enough to uproot the oldest.
A night went in prayers
and flute of the wind,
shadows of candles flickering,
like our intense fear.

Phase-3

The chaos of the night gave way,
to the morning sun.
Never so quiet a night had passed.
I was scared to my core to witness.
Such ruin it had proclaimed.

Toed towards the shore to know
what has become of our sail.
Hooked my palms tight to brothers hands
the fear yet to lose its grasp.

Found our friend washed to the shore.
The waves numbly foaming and returning.
Hands began to tremble as I tried to nudge.
Dragged I was away and not allowed.

Poetry Garden

Help came soon to treat him well,
took him in and siren the distance.

Went to him when the evening fell,
fragments of cans kept beside in a tray.

Poetry Garden

The forever strings

Phase-1

Hope the last night this will be.
To board this dimensional ride,
of these poignant emotions,
the emptiness, the void I feel,
not alone, but the whole house of ours.

Hope they will be leaving me tomorrow,
with you again by my side.
Yesterday when I was gazing,
at the ceiling of my midnight blues.

While I missed the smell of lilies you brought at night,
just tried to accept the truth, our half filled bed.
My solitude questioned, about you.
I just couldn't answer.

It knew after you came to this home,
and just made it like your own,
not a night has passed
that your warmth I have not felt.
Haven't felt without fear, just by holding your hand.

Poetry Garden

Haven't went to sleep while staring at your face.

Just when your bruises I remembered,
I so much craved for the wine I no longer seek.
When I thought about your space,
the venomous pain,
trying to break out in your tears.
It just scared me endlessly.

Phase-2

But when I closed my fingers tight I felt you,
the left hand ring it was,
the same platinum we both had in our finger.
When circled with conscience, it yielded faith.
It told me that you are fine.
It made my worries dust off, just like you made.

I felt somehow stringed to you,
no matter of our distance,
of all we have fought,
together,
of all the time was to come.
It gave me strength so firm.

Poetry Garden

Just when I could pragmatically feel
the happiness of your homecoming,
I went to dream of what more we can be,
how much more we can learn in love.

Poetry Garden

The game of possessions

Phase-1

In a corner unknown of an unseen street,
It caught my eye on the side of the glass.
Shimmered the beauty on the touch of such dusk.
An antique gramophone of uttered delicacy.

Thrashing the dissent on the pavement,
I went inside.
Just one lady I found.
Tactfully she bargained over a necklace.
Just a shade more from the clip,
defying with grace her bun of white.

The seller leaned and asked,
'what would be my interest?'
I aimed and it was brought to desk.

Never been a marvel at bargain.
But always thrived to be honest of foundation.
My wallet frowned when I splintered it sheer.
But I embraced the instrument I knew,
which had always elated us.

Poetry Garden

It's old peer had been forsaken.
It couldn't weave music anymore,
not even worthy to be dusted for its service.
The rich collection of records
summoned by the family,
just had been a stack of junk old.

Extravagance such instrument seemed,
with the crouching start-up I had,
but couldn't hold myself from feeling it again.
That music, that ambience,
it created with the daylight sneaking.

Phase-2

Might as well honour the pleasure,
of a serene birthday present.

When she opened the facade to find me,
holding the gramophone in a way awkward,
reminded her of the puppy I brought,
scuttling from school.

Poetry Garden

She just gave way to move in,
the silence being more tense
while the lock got fisted again.

Spilled all over the emotions,
just the moment next,
absurd and foolish she claimed,
but the stream of overwhelm diverged on its way.

By the time I was at the table,
for the morning tea routine.
Sima was just finishing off.

Phase-3

With the sound of peeling plastic,
the albums came out,
just as instructed by mother, I suppose.

Gracefully she set and clinched the harmony eternal,
the sensational feeling of a time long gone,
inhibited me from within.

Poetry Garden

The mornings felt different and full of life,
took in the emotions diving out of the rhythm.
It created an aura that swayed between years.

While tucking the netting one day
something disturbing she revealed.
A man had been lingering just astride the door,
but never he ventured to ring the call.
Yet gentle he appeared, she told.

phase-4

I finally witnessed on my own just a day after.
Restrained he looked as I stole a glimpse.
He looked sharp attired,
antagonized the assumptions I made,
I gathered the courage to attend.

Surprised me again when I found him
humming to the rhythm,
to the music which leaked,
through the windows.
He seemed stunned and puzzled at first,
but he eluded through my frowned glare.

Poetry Garden

Folded his hands to greet and smiled right to my face,
"Senior manager, tax department."
I read the appealing card in my mind,
just as if he handed me his distorted puzzle box.
He requested to come in and untangle,
just to reveal a story astonishing.

He told how he heard his grandfather, his song,
apologized for his tentative nature,
and proposed to buy the album.

He offered enough amount to save my diligence.
The man thrived for this album for a time long.
Since the one he had could not play again.
I had to tend my morals but it told me to trade.
If a past can save someone's present
and give future a enlightened chance.
Why not take it?
When it had arrived in the solace of wisdom.

Poetry Garden

The gift of snow

Phase-1

A special essence in the mist,
yet the day seemed like the other,
cloned reasons many had,
to leave the desk past two.

To share the warmth of lust,
fight the cold winds along.
To find and reach each other,
let it be for an occasion.

Like other days when the break time lured,
went up a mile where the mist is dense and fine,
where elated is a constant of state,
where a road has moulded
to a fun ground with time.

Shadows in pairs became visible when approached,
while the smoke of my cigar evanesce.
Many women came to my life,
none could I call my forever like them.
It hurts much, but on this day alone,

denser the cold became,
crave for warmth began to strive.

Poetry Garden

Came back to the place I belong,
where the wooden desk and it's mates
make me feel,
'It's just another day'.

The hours turned with pages of files,
the quieter it fell on the outside.
Leaned towards the desk to rest a while,
the next I knew it was way past light.

Phase-2

The window revealed the falling crystals.
Snow it was after a year of two.
After I came, to this hill of hope.

Embraced the gloves and clinched it tight,
flamed the headlight and started off,
persuaded the jacket the thin winds of cold,
while snow was clustering unpredictably, uneven.
A light intermittent of feature I could see,
Very close to the ground uncanny it seemed,

covered the distance in between,
a fallen ride was revealed.

Poetry Garden

The track of toy might have blocked the glide.
Cautious the person was, struggling.

Set free of her foot and face,
she gasped and looked horribly at me,
embellished a strive for a little water,
proven right was I of the subtle hint.

She spoke the native words,
but I was still a beginner,
yet, I could depict her bruises.

At the hospital I took her,
which mounted Just near my stay,
went to bed when the sun
was willing to day,
went to her when morning was gone.

phase-3

She slept while the sun dived through the window,
her hair like the first stream of mountain rain.
I was too puzzled to endure her the night other.
She was a very different form of gorgeous,
which was soothing and blazing.
when she woke up blinking twice.
It felt similar,
to the blooming of orchids pink.

Poetry Garden

Seven years have gone and it's snowing again,
the first time after that year.
But when it's time go back,
my little Cecilia still wants to play,
our daughter I should rather say.

Poetry Garden

It doesn't belong here

Phase-1

Being a magical endeavour this days seven past,
I wandered with the open suitcase.
Mother nature had been very kind and beautiful
towards me.
It's time to return again to the land of birth.
To the land my own.
To bid goodbye to the highway, delivering me
by the port to fly high.
Tempted by the wind spread on my face,
whispered to say, stay little longer.

Still I couldn't.
Had to break free of its surrealism held magically.
Never had I felt this blue after coming home.
Life returned to its norms with its native pace.
Been more than a week and the gloominess had damped.
Went to the garden to meet new members of the trees,
and feel fresh with the embracing green of tranquil.

Poetry Garden

Phase-2

After waving through the lilies, roses and
ascocendas born.
Drowsy I felt with the tired body.
Yet I perceived an unnatural pattern in my garden,
was bound to disregard my thoughts and melt in my bed.
Brewed the fresh coffee in the machine
and it smelled of the American south.
When the sky had been overcast,
by the obdurate star the brightest.

Left in a turmoil terrible with the heavy sound of a
thrash.
In the terrace that I saw the heavy tree crashed into the
walls.
With the bubbled coffee in my hand staring into the
window I sat.

Just couldn't persuade to the reason of such sudden fall.
By the clarity of the daylight I went to eye around.
Roots of the hardwood raised to the surface.
It's ruin of cracks wearing the terrace.
Oh lord, what abnormality did I witnessed the moment.

All the plants and even the giant trees
have crooked towards the pale house window.

Poetry Garden

I went inside terrified of such reality.
The roses down to the earth waiting
to crawl a little further.

Phase-3

The strong bough's reaching out with its empty hands.
All the stems directed towards the window.
Only when it thundered my mind,
brought along something maybe shouldn't have.
La serena seemed like a lighthouse much aged.

Never did I thought the moai
living by the stones is cursed.
In the backyard did I encountered it,
removing a grey block.
And I knew it's not an acclaimed work of the house.
In that evening another tree fell,
And the house trembled like my wit.
The shadows of them on the window telling me,
"We are not far now".

A tub of reflections

Poetry Garden

The street in which knowledge stumbles into passion is the enclave where the first brick of an empire is laid.

~~~~~~~~~~~~~~~~~~~~~~~~~

Learning to ride a bicycle holds a very bright lesson of life.
We often don't see it.
It teaches about acceptance at first.
It tells us it won't be easy, nothing is easy.
We should be willing to fall, attend the bruises.
And show up again, show some respect and get a little better.

~~~~~~~~~~~~~~~~~~~~~~~~~

The one thing we are taught from childhood is to be a good person. At some point of our lives we realize that it is not deceitful.

Poetry Garden

If you cannot respect the struggle, the fight,
the phase where nothing worth is achieved yet,
you should not expect any form of share of the
accomplishment and the tranquillity.

~~~~~~~~~~~~~~~~~~~~~~~~~~~

A decision taken in haste and without analyzing the ups
and downs, will often prove to be a decision which was
wrong.

~~~~~~~~~~~~~~~~~~~~~~~~~~~

The more you travel, the more you see,
the more you take in.
You will realize that travelling is more of a necessity than
an extravagance.

Poetry Garden

Inside every person there is a whole of a universe itself.
Sometime try to feel the stars and planets stirring inside
marvellously.

~~~~~~~~~~~~~~~~~~~~~~~~~~~

People subcautiously are attracted to things with which
they can connect somehow and thus relate.
Things which make them smile from the core even if it
fails to show on their countenance.
The attraction will be vividly different for different souls.
Much depending on the strength's and past experiences.

Poetry Garden

Even after we grow up we have still posses that strange habit of gaining from the people we mostly spend our time with.

~~~~~~~~~~~~~~~~~~~~~~~~~

When in pursuit for love, we should look for imperfections,
acceptable and tolerable imperfections.

~~~~~~~~~~~~~~~~~~~~~~~~~

Peculiarity is in how we always manage to keep things in a higher order which we don't have. The things we have always are undervalued in comparison.

Poetry Garden

Always try to help anyone you can. It would be hard in today's world expecting nothing in return. But let's still do it while we still can.
When we will help without expecting anything, we will make the other person believe that goodness is still in abundance and it would begin to reciprocate,
just right there from you.

~~~~~~~~~~~~~~~~~~~~~~~~~~~

Dreams are extraordinarily powerful. It makes us work harder like nothing else. It makes a person stronger and teaches how to fight for something. In other words it has the power of injecting life into us like nothing else.

Poetry Garden

Good morals and good manners will always open new doors for us. Some realizes a little sooner some realizes a little later.

~~~~~~~~~~~~~~~~~~~~~~~~~

There is a huge lack of appreciation of efforts everywhere. Efforts are not supplied much respect until success is finally received.
The appreciation should be flourishing. Encouragement should be tireless.

Poetry Garden

Everyone you have an attachment with no matter how close you are, deserves to have a small bubble of space for their own. It can be your wife, your sister, anyone. It's a peculiar vibe that you should know every bit of their thoughts, their doings. That it's their duty to let you be known of all of there is.

~~~~~~~~~~~~~~~~~~~~~~~~~

This ruins the identity, the respect they have for themselves. Don't venture or crash down into their everything. You might lose of all they are sharing and providing.
It's just not right to know a person's everything.

~~~~~~~~~~~~~~~~~~~~~~~~~

Never should you regret the voids made in you with age. It's a void which is not meant to be filled perpetually. It's like the space created for temporary people, so that they can stay and thus leave without any complexity.

page-59

Poetry Garden

It's very important to know what's best for you. Not what others think what's better, but what you think is better for your soul. What you need to do to level up your strengths and what you need to work on vigorously.

~~~~~~~~~~~~~~~~~~~~~~~~~~~

If something is stripping you off slowly of your originality if you feel like you are slowly losing the person you are, if it's ruining you for the worse, it should be abandoned while you still can.

~~~~~~~~~~~~~~~~~~~~~~~~~~~

It is necessary to ask yourself at the end of every day that- have you done enough of what matters?
This is how you will be able to reduce the trash out of daily life and increase the amount of things which matters.
It is very important to be respectable to yourself. It's the only person you cannot lie to.

Thank you for buying this book.
I hope that you enjoyed it.
Leave a review to let me know about your experience.

Author's email id:
trinankur.45@gmail.com

About the Publisher

Lightning Source UK Ltd.
Milton Keynes UK
UKHW010628200621
385805UK00001B/311